Tiny Toon Adventures, the Tiny Toon Adventures character names and likenesses are trademarks of Warner Bros. Inc. ©1990 Warner Bros. Inc. All Rights Reserved.

GOLDEN
®

A GOLDEN BOOK®
Western Publishing Company, Inc.
Racine, Wisconsin 53404

Help Buster and Babs find these nine things that they will use at school: a book, pencil, ruler, crayon, calculator, backpack, scissors, paints, and lunch.

Color Hamton and his home by using the color code.

1	BLACK	5	GREEN
2	BROWN	6	YELLOW
3	RED	7	WHITE
4	BLUE	8	PINK

Guide Plucky through the swamp to his home.

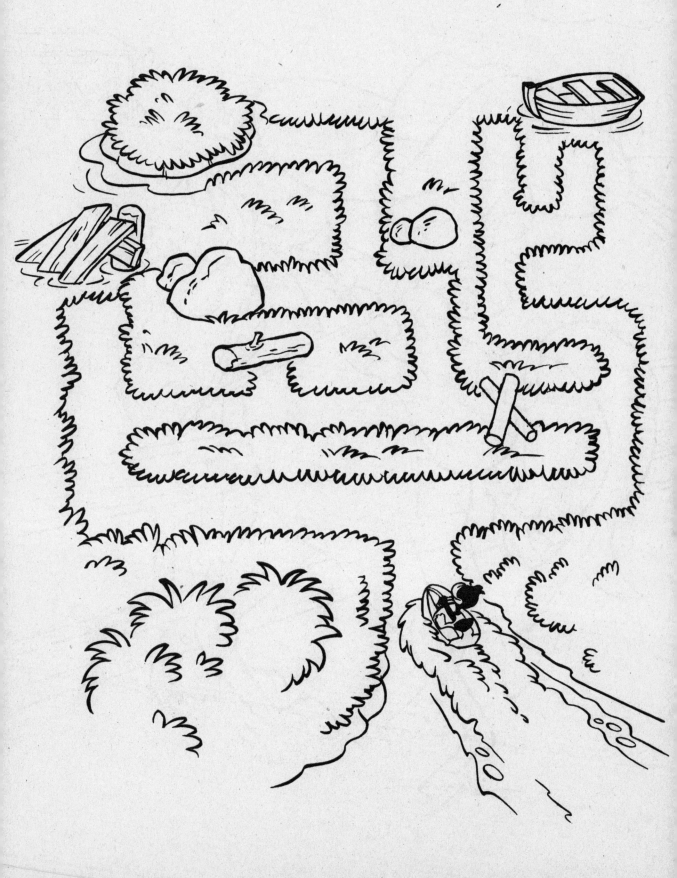

Ten of Elmyra's pets are hidden in the puzzle. Find a dog, cat, lamb, turtle, bunny, hamster, bird, puppy, kitten, and fish. Circle the words up, down, and across.

```
H  A  M  S  T  E  R  Y
O  D  X  G  V  F  I  N
P  L  N  O  H  I  Y  N
U  R  E  D  B  S  J  U
P  C  T  I  H  H  S  B
P  A  T  U  R  T  L  E
Y  T  I  Q  D  C  A  R
A  C  K  N  L  A  M  B
```

Draw a line from each object Dizzy has tasted to its description.

TOUGH & SOFT

ORANGE & CRUNCHY

HARD & HEAVY

ROUND & SWEET

TALL & HARD

ROUND & CHEWY

Find out if Buster is faster than Little Beeper. Each player places a coin in one of the lanes. Players take turns flipping another coin to move around the track. Move two spaces for tails and one space for heads. Players must follow the directions in the spaces they land on. The first player to cross the finish line wins.

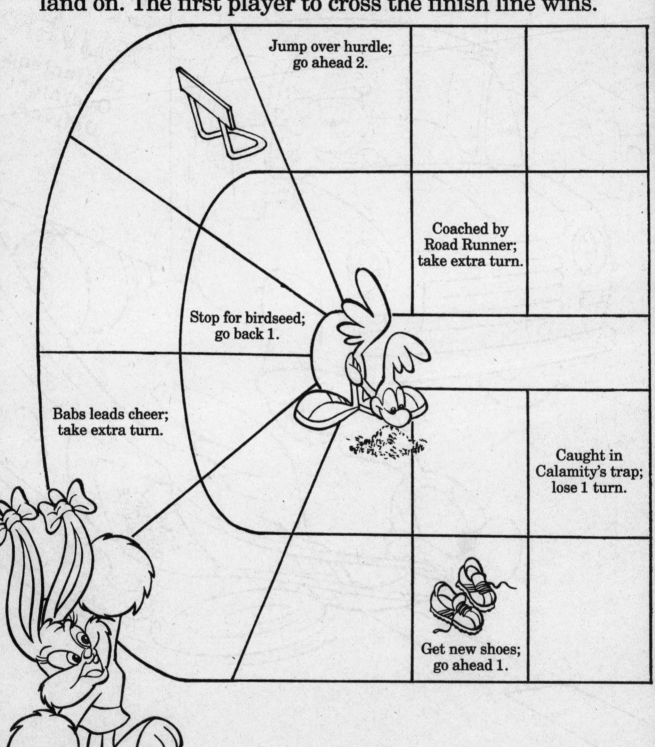

Jump over hurdle;
go ahead 2.

Coached by
Road Runner;
take extra turn.

Stop for birdseed;
go back 1.

Babs leads cheer;
take extra turn.

Caught in
Calamity's trap;
lose 1 turn.

Get new shoes;
go ahead 1.

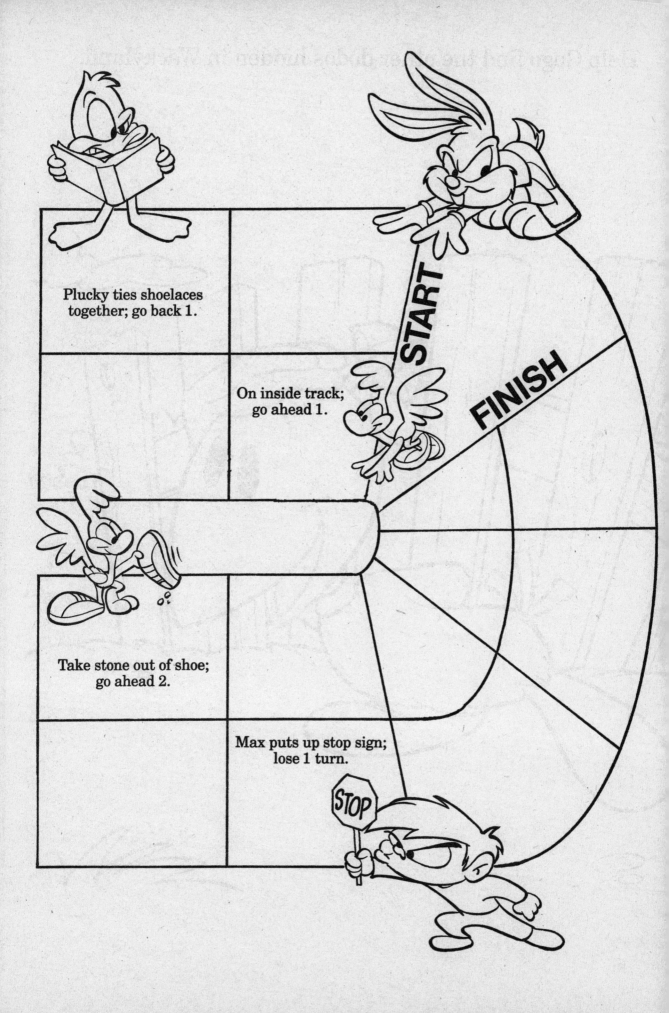

Plucky ties shoelaces together; go back 1.

On inside track; go ahead 1.

Take stone out of shoe; go ahead 2.

Max puts up stop sign; lose 1 turn.

START

FINISH

STOP

Help Gogo find the other dodos hidden in Wackyland.

Show Furrball the way out of the rain to his dry house.

Write the first letter of each object on the lines below to see what Sweetie is dreaming about.

___ ___ ___ ___ ___ ___ ___ ___

Connect the dots to see where Fifi lives.

Finish this picture of the animal that Bookworm is reading about.

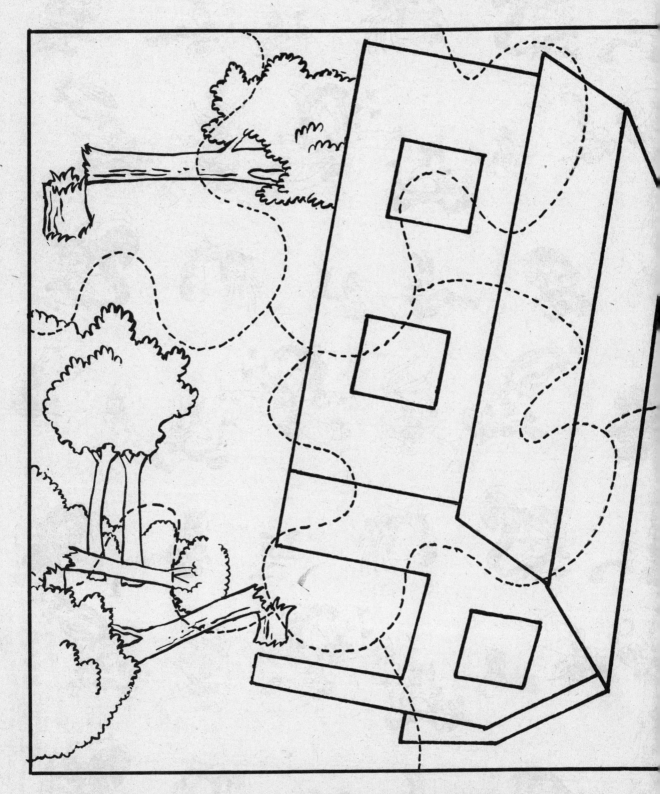

Cut out the page and glue it to light cardboard.
Color the pieces of the puzzle. Cut out the puzzle pieces.
Put together the building that Sneezer blew over.

To find out what Max likes best, write the correct letter above its number. The first letter is done for you.

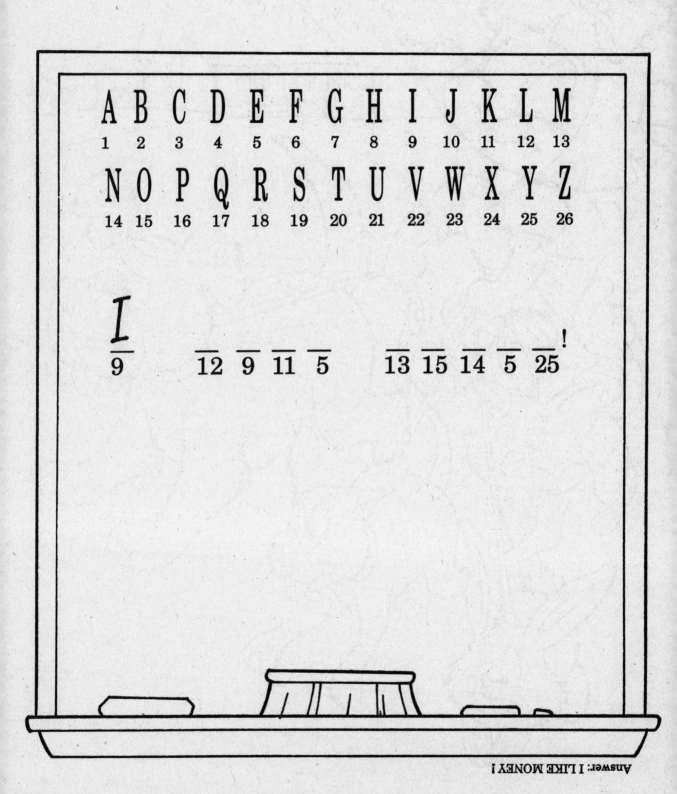

A B C D E F G H I J K L M
1 2 3 4 5 6 7 8 9 10 11 12 13

N O P Q R S T U V W X Y Z
14 15 16 17 18 19 20 21 22 23 24 25 26

I
—
9   ── ── ── ──   ── ── ── ── ──!
     12 9 11 5   13 15 14 5 25

Follow the leashes to find the pet that got away from Elmyra.

Babs, Shirley, and Fifi share things with one another. Color all the objects with a B one color, the ones with an S another color, and those with an F a third color. This will help the girls find their own items.

CROSS
. What you do with a game
. What you wear for trick or treat
. Type of television show featuring Tiny Toon characters

OWN
. What Babs likes to do with her feet
. What you read
. What you listen to on the radio
. What you watch while eating popcorn
. Another name for television

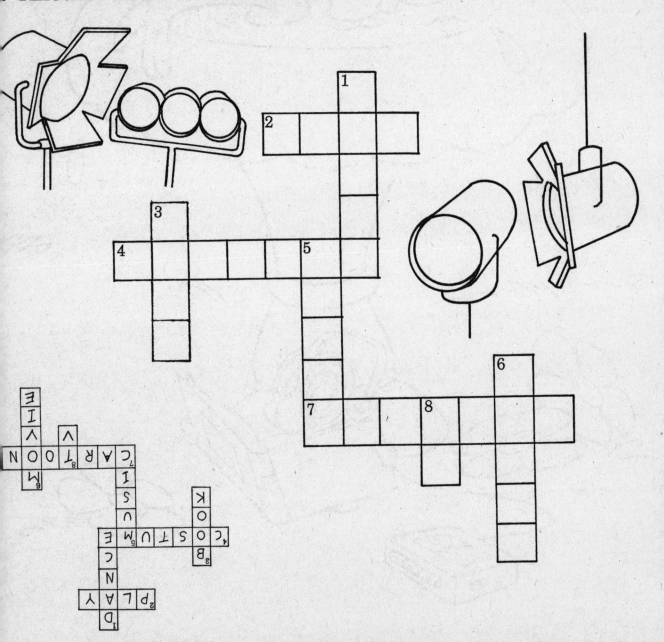

Paste these two pages to light cardboard and color the characters. Then cut out the characters and tape them to ice-cream sticks to make your own Tiny Toon puppets.

What five things are wrong with Calamity's bicycle?

To see Plucky fly and Gogo swim, turn the page upside down.

Can you draw a building like Acme Looniversity using triangles, circles, rectangles, and squares?

Hamton has taken enough food for the entire day. Sort his food into three meals for him. Mark breakfast food with a B, lunch with an L, and supper with an S.

se the code to write the correct letter above its number.

B C D E F G H I J K L M N O P Q R S T U V W X Y Z
2 3 4 5 6 7 8 9 10 11 12 13 14 15 16 17 18 19 20 21 22 23 24 25 26

_ _ _   _ _ _ _
20 8 5   19 8 15 23

_ _ _ _   _ _   _ _ !
13 21 19 20   7 15   15 14